To Katie, Ben & Bump.
D.L.

First published in Great Britain in 2017 by Frances Lincoln Children's Books,
The Old Brewery, 6 Blundell Street, London, N7 9BH, UK
QuartoKnows.com
Visit our blogs at QuartoKnows.com

Text and illustrations copyright © David Litchfield 2017

A catalogue record for this book is available from the British Library.

ISBN 978-1-84780-847-9

Illustrated digitally

Designed by Andrew Watson • Edited by Katie Cotton

Printed in China

5 7 9 8 6

GRANDAD'S SECRET
GIANT

David Litchfield

Frances Lincoln
Children's Books

Little Billy was in a pickle.
"Grandad," he said, "we've been painting the
town mural all day, but we just can't finish it!
No one can reach the top of the wall."

"Don't worry!" said Grandad.
"I know just the chap who can help..."

"He has hands the size of tables," Grandad continued, "legs as long as drainpipes, and feet as big as rowing boats. Do you know who I mean?"

"The secret giant," Billy sighed. "You've told me about him a thousand times, Grandad. You're making it up!"
"I never make things up," said Grandad.

"Do you remember when we went camping last summer?"
"Yes, Grandad," Billy groaned.

"The giant was there watching over us, making sure we kept safe."

"And do you remember when
the town clock was broken?"
"Yes, Grandad," Billy mumbled.

"It was the giant who fixed it," said Grandad.

"And do you remember when
our boat got caught in the storm?"
"Yes, Grandad," Billy sighed.

"It was the giant who pulled us safely to shore."
"But that's IMPOSSIBLE Grandad,"
Billy said. "I didn't see a giant!"
"Maybe you weren't looking hard enough," Grandad replied.

"And that's not all the giant's done. He also…

stopped the big oak from falling in the wind,

helped the cars cross the bridge when part of it fell down,

caught your kite before it blew away,

and rescued Murphy when he got stuck on the roof.

The giant does all these things for our town, quietly and
without making a fuss. And nobody knows except for me.
(You don't get to my age without sharp eyes.)"

"But Grandad," Billy said, "if the
giant is so helpful and good, why does
he want to stay such a BIG secret?"
"Because people are scared of things
that are different," said Grandad.

"When people see the giant, they
scream and run away. It makes him sad."
"I wouldn't be scared of a silly old giant,"
Billy scoffed.
"If he was real. Which he's NOT."
"Try getting up and going to the mural
tomorrow at dawn," Grandad said, with a wink.

The next morning, Murphy woke Billy up at dawn. He tried
to go back to sleep, but Murphy wouldn't stop barking.

So Billy decided to take him for a walk and to prove, once
and for all, that Grandad's secret giant wasn't real.

When they got closer to the mural,
Murphy whined nervously.
"Don't be daft, boy," said Billy
as they turned the corner.
"There's no such thing as a…"

"...G...G... GIANT!"

He WAS real...

he was HUMUNGOUS...

and he was
TERRIFYING!

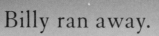
Billy ran away.

As fast as he could.

But then he had a thought.

Maybe this was what Grandad meant when he said people are scared of things that are different.

Billy turned back...

But the giant had gone.

Billy went to Grandad's and told him what had happened.

"I shouldn't have run away," he said sadly.
"Well, we all make mistakes sometimes," said Grandad,
"but I'm sure you can think of a way to make the giant feel better.
What makes you feel better when you're upset?"

Billy thought for a moment. Then, he had a great idea.

Billy told Grandad his plan,

and they got to work.

They hammered...

They sawed...

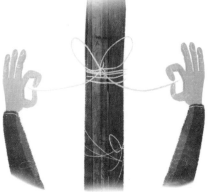

They worked hard all day to make the
giant a present he would never forget.

When it was finished, Billy and Grandad
hoisted Murphy up high, hoping the giant
would come and rescue him again.

Then there was nothing
to do but wait…

and wait some more.

They waited all afternoon,
until the sun began to set.

"What if the giant doesn't come back?" Billy said.
"Maybe he's fed up of people screaming and running away.
Maybe he doesn't want to live in our town because of me!"

But then ...

they saw legs as long as drainpipes, hands as big as table tops,
and feet as large as rowing boats.

IT WAS THE GIANT!

Just like they planned, he rescued Murphy from the ledge.
Then the giant saw the present.
For the first time since Grandad had known him, he smiled.

Because what Billy had realised was that the giant wasn't just a giant. He was also a person.

And he wanted what everyone
wanted when they were upset.

A friend.